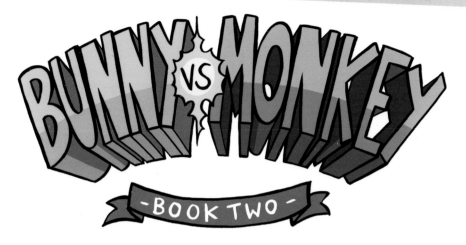

BUNNY VS MONKEY

- BOOK TWO -

BY JAMIE SMART

YEAR ONE
JULY - DECEMBER

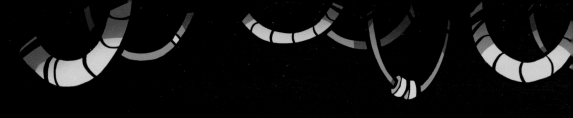

DEDICATED TO ALL THE WONDERFUL, BRILLIANT, AMAZING PHOENIX READERS!

Bunny vs Monkey: Book 2
is a
DAVID FICKLING BOOK

First published in Great Britain in 2015 by
David Fickling Books,
31 Beaumont Street,
Oxford, OX1 2NP
www.davidficklingbooks.com

Text and Illustrations © Jamie Smart, 2015

978-1-910200-47-6

7 9 10 8 6

David Fickling Books reg. no. 8340307

● A CIP catalogue record
for this book is available
from the British Library.

Printed and bound in Great Britain by Sterling.

Papers used by David Fickling Books are from
well-managed forests and other responsible sources.

CONTENTS!

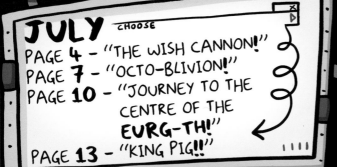

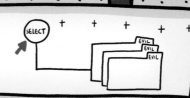

SELECT

+ + + + +

EVIL
EVIL
EVIL

JULY

-THE- WISH CANNON!

DEEP UNDERGROUND, IN SKUNKY'S SECRET LAIR...

Y'KNOW, SKUNKY, IT'S STRANGE. EVERY DAY I COME DOWN HERE AND SAY "QUICK, SKUNKY, I NEED AN INVENTION FOR A SPECIFIC TASK!" AND EVERY TIME, YOU JUST HAPPEN TO HAVE BEEN WORKING ON JUST THE RIGHT THING.

YOU MEAN, IT'S ALL A LITTLE TOO CONVENIENT? AS IF IT'S ALL TOO EASY?

WELL DON'T WORRY ABOUT THAT NOW. HAVE A GO ON MY NEWEST INVENTION, **THE WISH CANNON** INSTEAD!

OOOH!

THE WISH CANNON SYNTHETICALLY BONDS WITH THE DNA OF WHOEVER IS HOLDING IT, AND INTERPRETS THEIR BRAIN WAVES INTO OBJECTS, WHICH IT THEN PROPELS AT HIGH SPEED!

BASICALLY, IT FIRES **WHATEVER YOU WANT!**

WHAT ABOUT FIRE? DOES IT FIRE FIRE...? **WHOA!!**

FWOOSH!

MY LAB!

I BET IT CAN'T FIRE **HAM AND SAUERKRAUT!**

SPLAT!

SPLAT!

OH, WOULD YOU LOOK AT THAT.

ANYTHING, MONKEY. IT'S THE MOST ADVANCED WEAPON IN THE WORLD!

ABOVE GROUND...

BOW DOWN, WOODLAND IDIOTS! YOUR NEW LEADER MONKEY HOLDS ALL THE POWER NOW!

I'LL SWAP YOU THAT THING FOR THIS CAKE.

OOH, I DO LIKE CAKE.

4

WHERE, UM, WHERE IS THE WISH CANNON?

I DUNNO.

I LIKE CAKES.

EE HEE HEE! PEW PEW! HEE HEE! PEW!

TEE HEE! WHAT IS THAT THING?

I'M NOT SURE, BUT...

SPLAT!!

JELLY!

EEK! I'M SO SORRY!

PTOO!

MMM, DELICIOUS! IS IT A JELLY GUN? LET ME HAVE A GO!

HEE HEE, OKAY. SEE IF YOU CAN HIT ME.

KITTENS!!

OOPS!

PTOO! PTOO!

SHRIEK! KITTENS!

OHHH, SO IT'S A **KITTEN CANNON!** THAT'S FUNNY, I WAS JUST THINKING ABOUT KITTENS.

JUST DON'T FIRE IT AGAIN! WE NEED A GROWN UP!

WHAT'S GOING ON? I WAS JUST ABOUT TO GO TO THE TOILET.

P-TOOMPH!

OH, WE WERE HOPING YOU'D BE AROUND, BUNNY. THIS THING, IT KEEPS SHOOTING WEIRD STUFF AT US. WHATEVER WE THINK ABOUT!

A GUN WHICH FIRES WHATEVER YOU'RE THINKING, EH?

SOUNDS LIKE SOME SORT OF... **WISH CANNON!**

HOI! YOU GIVE THAT BACK!

STAND BACK, SKUNKY! I'M THINKING ABOUT SOME PARTICULARLY MOULDY SANDWICHES!

PAH! THINK YOU CAN DEFEAT ME WITH MY OWN INVENTION?

WHEN I HAVE THE **WISH CANNON DEFLECTOR SHIELD?** (WHICH I JUST INVENTED.)

THE WHAT?

5

OCTO-BLIVION!

AHHH.

THERE IS NOTHING, ABSOLUTELY NOTHING, BETTER THAN BEING A BUNNY IN A BOAT.

OH WAIT, NOW THAT'S BETTER. LOOKS LIKE I CAUGHT A BITE, TOO!

BLIP!

YEARGHH! OR RATHER, IT CAUGHT ME!!

H.M.S BUGS

VWOOOOM!!

NYEEEEEEEEEE!!

WHEW, YOU'RE A TRICKY LITTLE CUSTOMER, AREN'T YOU...

WHATEVER YOU ARE.

WHAT... ARE YOU?

JOURNEY TO THE CENTRE OF THE EURG-TH!

IT'S A BLISTERINGLY HOT DAY IN THE WOODS, AND ONE INHABITANT ISN'T ENJOYING IT...

MY SNOWMAN MELTED!!

A SNOWMAN? BUT IT HASN'T SNOWED FOR MONTHS... OH.

I MADE HIM OUT OF **CUSTARD.**

TECHNICALLY, HE'S A CUSTARD MAN.

SOB! GOODBYE, OLD FRIEND.

POOEY! SOMETHING SMELLS LIKE RANCID CUSTARD.

BOO HOO!

THIS HEAT IS MAKING LIFE VERY DIFFICULT FOR ALL OF US. LET'S JUST HOPE IT COOLS DOWN SOON.

!!

SOOO, THESE IDIOTS DON'T LIKE THE HEAT, EH? SO IF IT WAS EVEN HOTTER, THEY'D HAVE TO LEAVE, EH?

MEANING I COULD TAKE OVER THE WOODS! EH?

WE MUST MAKE IT HOTTER!

AND HOW DO WE DO THAT?

SIMPLE! WE CREATE A **VOLCANO**, BY BURROWING DOWN INTO THE CENTRE OF THE EARTH, AND FLOODING THE LAND WITH **MOLTEN LAVA!**

BUT HOW DO WE DO THAT?

YOU INVENT A **THING!**

SIGHHH. I SUPPOSE I'D BETTER GET STARTED, THEN.

HURRY UP! FIVE MINUTES!

KING PIG!!

IT'S THURSDAY, AND WEENIE AND PIG ARE BEING CREATIVE...

HEE HEE! I AM DRAWING AN ASTRONAUT GIVING AN ALIEN A KISS!

WHAT HAVE YOU DRAWN, PIG?

I HAVE DRAWN A **CROWN.** PARTLY BECAUSE I ONLY HAVE A YELLOW CRAYON.

I STUFFED ALL THE OTHERS UP MY NOSE.

GASP! IF YOU HAVE A CROWN, YOU KNOW WHAT THAT MEANS!

YES!

WAIT, NO.

IT MEANS YOU'RE A KING NOW!

ALL HAIL KING PIG!

ALL HAIL KING ME!

BUNNY! BUNNY! PIG HAS BEEN CROWNED **KING!**

REALLY?

LEGALLY?

IS HE WEARING MY CURTAINS?

WE EVEN WROTE A LIST OF THINGS KINGS DO!

HMM WELL, THIS ALL SEEMS PRETTY COMPREHENSIVE.

WHAT DO YOU WANT TO DO FIRST?

UMM...

KING THINGS
1. LIVE IN A CASTLE
2. HOLD BANQUETS
3. MAKE LAWS

NEXT TIME - "FANTASTIQUE LE FOX!"

15

AUGUST

FANTASTIQUE LE FOX!

GOOD MORNING, LE FOX. WE DON'T OFTEN SEE YOU WALKING AROUND.

HARUMPH.

DON'T TALK TO ME.

THAT'S A BIT RUDE. I WAS ONLY BEING FRIENDLY, WHY DO YOU HAVE TO BE SO GRUMPY ALL THE TIME?

SIGH.

YOU WANT TO KNOW WHY, LITTLE BUNNY? YOU WANT TO KNOW THE HORRORS I'VE SEEN?

UM. NOT SURE NOW.

I PARACHUTED INTO THESE WOODS A LONG, LONG TIME AGO, BEFORE YOU WERE EVEN BORN, IN THE MIDST OF WAR!

MY JOB WAS TO RECLAIM THE AREA FOR THE ALLIES. I DID SO USING STEALTH, TACTICS AND BIG EXPLOSIONS.

BOOM!!

SINCE THEN, I HAVE REMAINED HERE. SUFFERING THROUGH YEARS OF COLD, LONELINESS AND MISERY, TO ENSURE THESE WOODS ARE NEVER INVADED AGAIN.

SO YOU ASK ME WHY I AM GRUMPY.

HOW DARE YOU.

GOSH, I HAD NO IDEA.

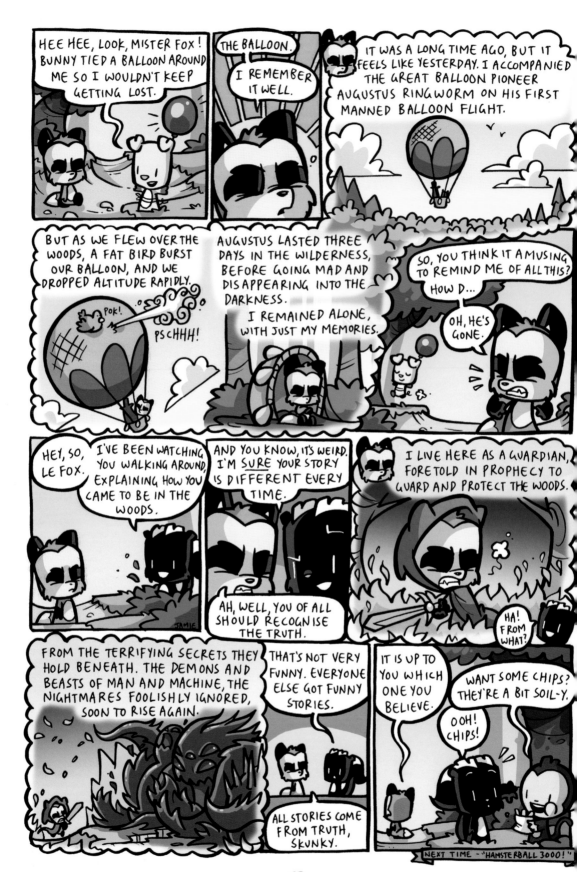

HEE HEE, LOOK, MISTER FOX! BUNNY TIED A BALLOON AROUND ME SO I WOULDN'T KEEP GETTING LOST.

THE BALLOON. I REMEMBER IT WELL.

IT WAS A LONG TIME AGO, BUT IT FEELS LIKE YESTERDAY. I ACCOMPANIED THE GREAT BALLOON PIONEER AUGUSTUS RINGWORM ON HIS FIRST MANNED BALLOON FLIGHT.

BUT AS WE FLEW OVER THE WOODS, A FAT BIRD BURST OUR BALLOON, AND WE DROPPED ALTITUDE RAPIDLY.

POK!

PSCHHH!

AUGUSTUS LASTED THREE DAYS IN THE WILDERNESS, BEFORE GOING MAD AND DISAPPEARING INTO THE DARKNESS.

I REMAINED ALONE, WITH JUST MY MEMORIES.

SO, YOU THINK IT AMUSING TO REMIND ME OF ALL THIS? HOW D...

OH, HE'S GONE.

HEY, SO, LE FOX.

I'VE BEEN WATCHING YOU WALKING AROUND, EXPLAINING HOW YOU CAME TO BE IN THE WOODS.

AND YOU KNOW, IT'S WEIRD. I'M SURE YOUR STORY IS DIFFERENT EVERY TIME.

AH, WELL, YOU OF ALL SHOULD RECOGNISE THE TRUTH.

I LIVE HERE AS A GUARDIAN, FORETOLD IN PROPHECY TO GUARD AND PROTECT THE WOODS.

HA! FROM WHAT?

FROM THE TERRIFYING SECRETS THEY HOLD BENEATH. THE DEMONS AND BEASTS OF MAN AND MACHINE, THE NIGHTMARES FOOLISHLY IGNORED, SOON TO RISE AGAIN.

THAT'S NOT VERY FUNNY. EVERYONE ELSE GOT FUNNY STORIES.

IT IS UP TO YOU WHICH ONE YOU BELIEVE.

WANT SOME CHIPS? THEY'RE A BIT SOIL-Y.

OOH! CHIPS!

ALL STORIES COME FROM TRUTH, SKUNKY.

NEXT TIME - "HAMSTERBALL 3000!"

18

HAMSTERBALL 3000!

WHAT INCREDIBLE BEAST IS THIS, RACING THROUGH THE WOODS AT SIXTY MILES AN HOUR (APPROX)?

VMMM!

VMMMMM!

VMMMMM!

WHAT MISCHIEVOUS SPRITE TEARS PAST THE OTHER ANIMALS?

MY BUNS!

VMMMMMMM!

WHAT DANGER DISRUPTS THE PEACE AND QUIET OF THE WOODLAND?

BOP!

BOP!

VMMM!

OW!

OW!

WHAT DEVIOUS INVENTION HAS SKUNKY CREATED THIS TIME?

VMMM!

IT'S NOT ONE OF MINE!

VMMM!

OH, SORRY.

THEN IT MUST BE THE NEW, AERODYNAMICALLY-IMPROVED...

HAMSTERBALL 3000!

VMMM!

MEEP MEEP!

WHAT IS IT?

I WANT ONE!

A HAMSTER BALL? YOU WOULDN'T FIT.

SCREECH!

A SALAD SANDWICH! THAT LOOKS TASTY, CAN I HAVE SOME? SAVES YOU EATING IT.

MEEP!

ARE YOU MY CONSCIENCE?

NO, SILLY! I'M A HAMSTER! HAMSTERS EAT SALAD!

ROLL...BONK!

MMM, SALAD.

IT WON'T GO THROUGH YOUR FORRRCE-FIELD!

AWW, MEEP!

PUFF...HI THERE! I'M BUNNY, WELCOME TO OUR WOODS!

SQUELCH!

I'M PIPI! I'VE BEEN RUNNING AND RUNNING AND RUNNING FOR SO LONG, I'M NOT EVEN SURE WHERE I AM!

MEEP!

I SURE LOVE RUNNING.

WELL, YOU'RE WELCOME TO STAY HERE, WITH US, IF YOU LIKE.

OH I CAN'T DO THAT. THEY'RE COMING!

MEEP!

WHO ARE?

YOU KNOW WHO.

AHH! YOU'RE GOING TO BE VERY USEFUL, WEIRD MOUSE-IN-A-BALLOON THING.

GRAB!

MEEP!

MONKEY, WAIT! HE HAD SOMETHING TO TELL US!

TOO LATE! RODENT McSPEEDY PANTS IS JUST WHAT SKUNKY NEEDS FOR HIS NEW INVENTION!

MEEP!

WHAT INVENTION?

I DUNNO, COME UP WITH SOMETHING!

OHHH.

A LITTLE BIT LATER...

I MISS PIPI. HE WAS FUNNY. AND SMALL.

AND FUNNY.

HE CERTAINLY WAS INTRIGUING.

I LIKED IT WHEN HE RAN! HEE HEE! I LIKED THAT BIT TOO!

HEE HEE!

RUN RUN RUN!

SHH! DO YOU HEAR SOMETHING?

NO.

OH. I THOUGHT I DID.

BEE-DAY!

BUZZ BUZZ!

BUZZ OOMPH!

BUZZ BUZZ!!

WHAT'S WRONG WITH YOU ALL? STOP IT!

BUT IT'S BEE-DAY, MISTER MONKEY!

BIDET?

BEE-DAY IS WHEN WE ALL DRESS UP LIKE FUNNY FUZZY BEES, AND CELEBRATE BEES BECAUSE BEES MAKE HONEY.

BECAUSE HONEY IS YUMMY!

WELL, YOU'RE ALL STILL STUPID. VERY WELL DONE. I REFUSE TO BE INVOLVED IN YOUR SILLY BEE-DAY.

OKEE DOKEE! BUZZZZ! HEE HEE!

I CHANGED MY MIND! AND I BROUGHT SOME GUESTS OF HONOUR!

I STOLE THEM OFF A TREE.

A BEE HIVE!

WHAT'S YOUR PROBLEM? I THOUGHT YOU ALL LIKED BEES.

WE DO. THAT'S WHY WE WOULDN'T DISTURB THEIR HIVE!

YOU'RE GONNA MAKE THEM...

...ANGRY.

RUMMMMMBLE!

THERE. YOU ARE NEARER. NOW WHAT?

HMM, I'M STILL GOING TO GET STUNG IF I GO OUT THERE.

BUT **ACTION BEAVER** COULD DO IT!

HE RELISHES DANGER!

BUZZ! BUZZ BUZZ!

ACTION BEAVER! PSST! WE NEED YOU TO PUT THIS BEE HIVE BACK ON ITS TREE!

BZZ? FWIBBLE.

BURP!

YES! EXACTLY!

CHOMP!!

NO! DON'T **EAT** IT!

HAR HAR, HE'S BECOME A BEE CANNON! WHAT FUN.

ACTION BEAVER, COME BACK! YOU'RE NOT HELPING!

PYEW! PYEW!

NOW HE'S FALLEN INTO LE FOX'S TUNNELS. OH ACTION BEAVER, YOU'RE SUCH A SILLY.

TUMBLE!

HANG ON...

INTO THE...

TUNNELS?

AUGH!! GET AWAY, YOU CRAZY THING! DON'T **BRING THE BEES TO US!**

INSIDE ACTION BEAVER'S BRAIN...

BUZZ BUZZ BUZZ BUZZ BUZZY BUZZ BUZZ **BRING THE BEES TO US!**

FLUMP!

P-TOO!!

FWINGGG!

PLOP!

PHEW! THE HIVE IS BACK, THE BEES ARE HAPPY, AND WE'RE ALL SAFE.

YOU'RE RIGHT, IT'S **BORING! LET'S DO IT AGAIN!**

NEXT TIME - "ACTION BEAVER²"

JAMIE

24

25

SEPTEMBER

GONE WITH THE WIND!

EEEK! BUNNY, WHY IS IT SO **WINDY** TODAY?

I DON'T KNOW, IS THIS ONE OF SKUNKY'S INVENTIONS?

NNNOPE.

IT MUST BE SUMMER COMING TO AN END. ALL MY WASHING IS GETTING BLOWN AROUND!

HANG ON, WHY DO YOU HAVE A TROLLEY OF CAKES?

DURING THE YEAR, I HIDE CAKES ALL ACROSS THE WOODS, IN CASE I NEED THEM IN AN EMERGENCY.

NOW AUTUMN'S ON ITS WAY, I NEED TO GATHER THEM ALL UP, AND STORE THEM BACK IN MY HOUSE.

EXCEPT THEY'RE BLOWING ALL OVER THE PLACE!

I MADE THEM TOO LIGHT!

SORRY, WEENIE, I REALLY NEED TO GATHER UP MY WASHING. I'LL HELP WHEN I'M DONE!

CHOMP! CHOMP! CHOMP!

PIG! STOP EATING MY WINTER STORES!

HEY, WHAT'S THIS WHITE SHEET? IS IT A GHOST WHO FELL OUT OF A PLANE?

OH, THAT MUST BE ONE OF BUNNY'S. WE SHOULD...

...TELL HIM **LATTTER.**

PLAN FORMING!

29

I, ROBOT CROCODILE!

As summer nears an end in the woods, what a beautiful time to take a walk and...

DESTROY!

BZZT!

METAL STEVE, STOP DOING THAT! YOU CAN'T JUST GO AROUND TEARING EVERYTHING APART.

BOP!

¡¡dOOHM

DESTROY!

BZZT!

YOU WOULD BE WISE NOT TO ANGER THE ROBOT, LITTLE BUNNY.

BUT HE HAS NO RIGHT!

BZZT!

I'M AFRAID SOME CREATURES JUST WANT TO SMASH EVERYTHING UP.

PAH! IF WE WORK TOGETHER, WE CAN ALL SHOW METAL STEVE HOW BEAUTIFUL AND PRECIOUS LIFE CAN BE!

BZZT! BZZT! BZZT!!

STEVE! HEY, STEVE! LOOK AT THESE LOVELY FLOWERS!

NO! THEY'RE NOT FOR YOU TO STOMP ON!

STOMP! STOMP!

NO STOMPING!

STOMP!

THERE'S A MOOSE LOOSE!

WOO WOO BONK OOF!!

SHRIEK! IT'S MONKEY!

GO AWAY! YOU'LL SPOIL IT!

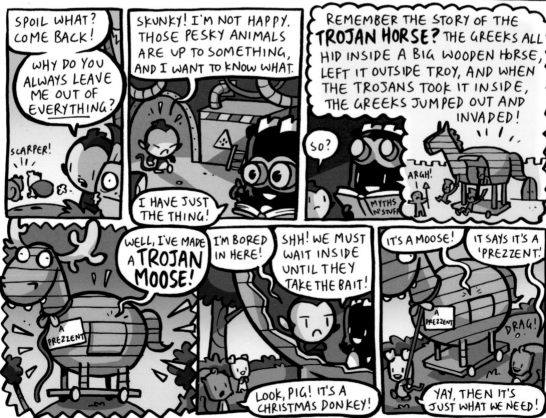

SPOIL WHAT? COME BACK!

WHY DO YOU ALWAYS LEAVE ME OUT OF EVERYTHING?

SCARPER!

SKUNKY! I'M NOT HAPPY. THOSE PESKY ANIMALS ARE UP TO SOMETHING, AND I WANT TO KNOW WHAT.

I HAVE JUST THE THING!

REMEMBER THE STORY OF THE **TROJAN HORSE?** THE GREEKS ALL HID INSIDE A BIG WOODEN HORSE, LEFT IT OUTSIDE TROY, AND WHEN THE TROJANS TOOK IT INSIDE, THE GREEKS JUMPED OUT AND INVADED!

SO?

ARGH!

MYTHS N' STUFF

WELL, I'VE MADE A **TROJAN MOOSE!**

A PREZZENT

I'M BORED IN HERE!

SHH! WE MUST WAIT INSIDE UNTIL THEY TAKE THE BAIT!

LOOK, PIG! IT'S A CHRISTMAS DONKEY!

IT'S A MOOSE!

IT SAYS IT'S A 'PREZZENT.'

A PREZZENT

DRAG!

YAY, THEN IT'S JUST WHAT WE NEED!

CONKER BONKERS!

ONCE A YEAR, THE BIGGEST HORSE CHESTNUT TREE IN THE WOODS RELEASES ITS BOUNTY...

CONKERS? WHAT'S SO SPECIAL ABOUT **CONKERS**?

WE THREAD THEM THROUGH STRING, AND DO BATTLE!

POW!

HEE HEE!

SMASH!

HMM...

OKAY, FINE! I WILL JOIN IN. BUT I DEMAND THE BIGGEST CONKER!

OH, THE BIGGEST ARE AT THE TOP OF THE TREE. NONE OF US CAN REACH THEM.

HERE, MONKEY, YOU CAN HAVE MY STARTER CONKER. I CALL IT...

...THE **TIDDLER!**

WHAT?

COME ON, MONKEY, I THOUGHT YOU WANTED TO JOIN IN!

YEAH, GAME ON, MONKEY!

HEE HEE!

GNNHH!!

ONE QUICK CONKER BATTLE LATER...

BAH! THEY ALL BEAT ME, AND MADE ME CRY. I AM THE <u>MONKEY</u>, I SHOULD HAVE THE MOST POWERFUL CONKER IN THE WOODS!

WELL, I JUST HAPPEN TO HAVE BEEN USING GENETIC MODIFICATION TO GROW SUCH A THING!

IT'S READY TO CRACK OUT OF ITS HUSK.

NO! LEAVE IT AS IT IS.

IT'S...PERFECT!

ACTION PIG!

NO, ACTION BEAVER CAN <u>NOT</u> COME OUT TO PLAY. HE SPENT ALL YESTERDAY JUMPING IN THE RIVER, AND NOW HE HAS A HIGH FEVER.

HOME SWEET HOME

Bobble... Fft! Fft! Schhh...

ICE PACK

#1

AWW. WHO'S GOING TO TEST-DRIVE MY LATEST INVENTION, THE **DRAGONFLY 5000**, NOW?

BZZZ!

HMMMM... I WONDER.

WHEEE! HA HA!

PIG, HOW WOULD YOU... UH... WHAT ARE YOU DOING?

I'M TRYING TO CATCH JELLY ON MY HEAD!

SPLAT?

<u>DID</u> IT.

CAN I ASK WHY?

I, UM... OH. I FORGOT.

HE'S PERFECT!

PIG, HOW WOULD YOU LIKE A LIFE OF ADVENTURE, DANGER AND EXCITEMENT?

WILL IT HURT?

YES! BUT IT WILL ALSO BE VERY FUNNY.

OH, I <u>DO</u> LIKE FUNNY THINGS.

THEN FROM THIS DAY FORTH, YOU SHALL BE OUR... **ACTION PIG!!**

THUNK!!

PYEW!

AUTUMN ARRIVES IN THE WOODS, AS THE LEAVES FALL FROM THE TREES, AND BUNNY SWEEPS THEM UP...

I MUST SAY, I FIND IT VERY RELAXING, DOING THIS.

THERE. A NICE, TIDY, PILE OF LEAVES.

OOMPH!

MY LEAVES! PIG, WHAT ARE YOU DOING?

I SAW A FLUTTER-BYE COME THIS WAY! I WANT TO BE ITS FRIEND!

C'MERE, MISSUS FLUTTER-BYE!

WE CAN PLAY FOOTBALLS!

SIGH. GUESS I'LL START AGAIN.

A BIT LATER...

THERE! HOPEFULLY THIS PILE WILL...

WHEEE! HAHA!

NOOOO!

38

DUCK RACE!

I DONE A BAD THING!!

BEWOOOO
BEEWOO
BEWOOO
BEWOOO

SKUNKY'S SECRET LAIR
SHHHH!

WHAT? WHAT DID YOU DOOO?

YOU KNOW AT THE BACK OF YOUR LAIR IS A DOOR MARKED 'B'? AND I WAS NOT, **UNDER ANY CIRCUMSTANCES**, TO OPEN DOOR B?

BECAUSE IT HELD MY **BIGGEST SECRET**, ONE WHICH WOULD **DESTROY US ALL**? YES?

YES?

I OPENED DOOR B.

ARGH!

I THOUGHT YOUR BIGGEST SECRET MIGHT BE **BISCUITS**.

I ONLY OPENED IT A LITTLE BIT, THEN ALL THESE ALARMS WENT OFF, AND I RAN.

WELL, **KEEP RUNNING!**

HEY, WHERE ARE YOU TWO GOING?

I OPENED DOOR B AND NOW WE'RE ALL DOOMED, SO WE'RE RUNNING AWAY.

OH. WELL, GOOD LUCK GETTING ACROSS THE FROZEN RIVER!

FORTUNATELY FOR US BOTH, OUR ESCAPE IS ALREADY TETHERED OVER THERE!

WHAT IS IT?

QUUAAAACK!!

~LORD~
QUACK-
QUACK!

MY NEW PROTOTYPE RUBBER DUCK, AQUATIC VEHICLE, AND ICE CRUSHER!

WE'LL BE ON OUR WAY IN NO TIME!

HANG ON. YOU CAN'T JUST LEAVE US HERE!

CRA-A-ACK!

CRIPES! THEY'RE AFTER US!

RELEASE DECOYS!

QUACK! QUACK! QUACK! QUACK! QUACK! QUACK!

EEE! DUCKIES!

PHEW! I HOPED THAT WOULD CONFUSE THEIR RADARS, AND IT DID!

QUACK ATTACK

BOOP!

IS IT BATHTIME?

AWAY WE GO, TO SAFETYYY!!

WOOHOO! SAFETY!

PLUMMET!

THEY'RE ODD, THOSE TWO.

LOOK! THEY LEFT THE LAIR OPEN!

I'VE NEVER BEEN IN THERE BEFORE. IS THERE HORROR INSIDE?

EEE!

QUACK!

JAMIE

MONKEY MENTIONED A "DOOR B".

AND I WANT TO KNOW WHAT IT IS.

GASP! FOLLOW OUR INNOCENT HEROES INSIDE IN PART 2 - "DOOR B"

NOVEMBER

DOOR ~B~

SKUNKY'S LAIR. HOME TO SOME OF THE MOST BIZARRE AND NIGHTMARISH CREATIONS YET TO WALK THE EARTH. A MYSTERIOUS CAVERN OF INVENTION AND DISCOVERY, SHROUDED IN SHADOW. FEW ENTER THIS PLACE, EVEN FEWER LEAVE.

WELCOME!
(PLEASE GO AWAY)

ONLY CERTAIN SOULS WOULD EVER CONTEMPLATE VENTURING INSIDE...

THE BRAVE.

COME ON, WE DON'T HAVE LONG.

THE HUNGRY.

I BROUGHT A QUICHE FOR EMERGENCIES!

THE UNDENIABLY STUPID.

WHEN I WALK FAST, I KICK MYSELF IN THE FACE!

HEE HEE!

FOCUS, YOU TWO. MONKEY SAID THE WOODS WERE IN DANGER, AND THAT IT WAS SOMETHING TO DO WITH **"DOOR B".**

WE MUST FIND IT.

IS IT LIKE A BEE MADE OF DOORS?

A DOOR BEE?

HEE HEE!

YOU'RE NOT HELPING.

42

Panel 1: WHAT ABOUT THIS, BUNNY? HAVE I FOUND IT?

THAT'S A MECHANICAL GORILLA SUIT, WEENIE.

Panel 2: LOOK AT ME! I'M A ROCKET PIG!

THAT'S SO MUCH FUN! LET'S SET YOU OFF!

STOP MESSING ABOUT.

Panel 3: WOOOOOSH!!

woosh.

woosh.

RIGHT, BUNNY. LOOKS LIKE IT'S JUST UP TO YOU TO FIND "DOOR B".

Panel 4: OH.

THERE IT IS.

Panel 5: WHAT'S IN HERE THAT SCARED EVEN SKUNKY SO MUCH?

WHAT HORRIBLE SECRET LIES INSIDE?

Panel 6: SORRY BUNNY, THAT'S NOT FOR YOU TO FIND OUT.

SLAM!

SKUNKY? I THOUGHT YOU WERE RUNNING AWAY WITH MONKEY!

Panel 7: I SUSPECTED CURIOUSITY WOULD GET THE BETTER OF YOU. WHAT IS THROUGH "DOOR B" IS NOT DANGEROUS IN ITSELF. ONLY IF <u>MONKEY</u> GETS TO IT WILL IT DESTROY THE WORLD.

SO, I HAD TO GET HIM AWAY. HE IS DISTRACTED BY TETHERBALL.

Panel 8: POK!

Panel 9: BUNNY! ROCKET PIG DOESN'T HAVE ANY BRAKES!

BOO HOO HOO.

YOU SHOULD GO, BUNNY. TAKE YOUR FRIENDS BACK TO THE SURFACE.

FORGET THIS EVER HAPPENED.

Panel 10: SOMETIMES, EVEN THE BRAVE, HUNGRY AND STUPID MUST WAIT FOR THEIR ANSWERS...

Panel 11: BECAUSE THE BIGGEST SECRETS ARE WELL PROTECTED.

Panel 12: AND THEY'RE THE ONES WHICH ARE BEST LEFT UNKNOWN.

FOR NOW...

JAMIE

NEXT TIME - "HYPNO-MONKEY!"

43

HYPNO-MONKEY!

It's a rare sunny day for this time of year, so Skunky has decided to take his work outside...

HEY, SKUNKY, WHAT'S THIS? I FOUND IT. CAN I KICK IT?

HMM?

$x = 5\frac{723}{19}$ $55703 / 19N + \sqrt{!!a + 90}$ WOO WOO

$BB \times 71111$

$012 + 17$

7

$15 w \times 9 \rightarrow$!!!

$2,000,000$ $27009 + 15^2$

$7777 \times FFF \div 23$

$BUM \sqrt{\frac{1555}{009}} \times YC + MM + = ?$

NO, MONKEY, PUT THAT DOWN. I AM CURRENTLY RESOLVING THE MOST COMPLICATED EQUATION KNOWN TO SCIENCE!

THE LAST THING I NEED IS YOU FIRING THAT AT ME.

WHY, WHAT IS IT?

IT IS A **MEMORY RAY.** IT RESETS THE BRAIN OF WHOEVER YOU FIRE IT AT!

SNATCH!

WIPES OUT THE MEMORIES.

LOOK, SEE?

ZZZAP!

YYYOINK!

WHAT AM I DOING HERE? LAST I REMEMBER, I WAS ON THE TOILET.

GOOD, MAYBE NOW YOU'LL LEAVE ME IN PEACE.

HANG ON A MINUTE. MONKEYS DON'T USE TOILETS.

SKUNKY, WHAT DOES THAT RAYGUN DO?

YOU DON'T REMEMBER? OH, OF COURSE YOU DON'T. HAHA!

HOI! SKUNKY! I KNOW WHAT YOU DID!

45

MONSTER PANTS!

IN THE DARKEST, SCARIEST CORNER OF THE WOODS, THREE INNOCENT FRIENDS TELL EACH OTHER THE MOST FRIGHTENING STORIES THEY KNOW...

AND THEN... **I FELL OVER!**

WOOOO.

WHAT, THAT'S IT? YOUR WHOLE STORY WAS THAT YOU FELL OVER? PIG, THAT'S NOT A SCARY STORY.

I LANDED ON MY NOSE.

HEE HEE. THAT'S A **FUNNY** STORY.

MY STORY WAS WAY SCARIER. THE ONE ABOUT A **GHOST'S GHOST.** EVEN **I** DON'T KNOW HOW THAT WORKS.

WOOO OOOO.

WAIT, I STILL HAVE A STORY!

I'M GUESSING IT HAS SOMETHING TO DO WITH THESE PANTS YOU MADE US WEAR?

NO. HEE HEE... **OKAY, YES!**

I'M GOING TO TELL YOU THE TERRIFYING TALE OF...

MONSTER PANTS!

AAAARGH!

OOH! I SCARED MYSELF!

I'LL BE HONEST, WEENIE. PANTS AREN'T USUALLY VERY SCARY.

I DON'T WANT TO HEAR ANY MORE SCARY STORIES.

OH, BUT THESE PANTS WERE. IN FACT, THEY WERE EVEN MORE FRIGHTENING THAN A GHOST'S GHOST OR PIG FALLING OVER.

IT ALL BEGAN WHEN I WAS A YOUNGER SQUIRREL.

I'D HEARD RUMOURS OF MONSTER PANTS, OF COURSE. BUT NOTHING COULD PREPARE ME FOR WHAT I WAS TO MEET THAT NIGHT...

LA LA LA.

A GIANT PAIR OF PANTS, ALL ANGRY AND GNASHING ITS TEETH!

I WAS SCARED AND RAN AWAY.

BUT IT CHASED ME! ALL THROUGH THE WOODS, TRYING TO BITE MY TAIL OFF.

I ONLY ESCAPED BY HIDING IN MANURE.

WEENIE! THAT NEVER HAPPENED!

IT DID! IT DID HAPPEN!

IN FACT, EVEN TO THIS DAY...

...YOU CAN STILL HEAR MONSTER PANTS CHOMPING DOWN TREES!

WEENIE! YOUR PANTS! THEY'RE BALLOONING!

FWIPPP!

NO... NO IT CAN'T BE...

SQUEAL!! I WAS WEARING MONSTER PANTS ALL ALONG!

FWOOOOP!

IT'S THE HOT AIR FROM THE FIRE, WEENIE! IT'S INFLATING YOUR PANTS!

SHRIIIIEK!

THEY'RE MORE BOXER SHORTS THAN PANTS ANYWAY.

I WANT TO GO HOME.

ARGH! MONSTER PANTS!

NEXT TIME - "BAD INFLUENCE!"

BAD INFLUENCE!

BUNNY! WE GOT STUCK IN A HOLE AGAIN!

SIGHHH.

WE'RE NOT SURE WHAT HAPPENED.

I'M TIRED OF BEING THE GROWN-UP TO YOU TWO. YOU NEED TO START LOOKING AFTER YOURSELVES.

I WAS LOOKING AFTER PIG.

AND I WAS LOOKING AFTER WEENIE.

WELL, JUST <u>TRY</u> TO NOT GET LOST, BURIED, BLOWN UP, OR ANYTHING ELSE THAT I'LL HAVE TO COME AND RESCUE YOU FROM.

OKAY?

WE'VE BEEN NAUGHTY.

VERY NAUGHTY.

NAUGHTY US.

HELLO!

IF YOU TWO ARE THE NEW TROUBLEMAKERS ROUND HERE, MAYBE WE SHOULD TEAM UP! POOL OUR RESOURCES!

LIKE A GANG?

WE COULD BE A GANG!

HOW EXCITING! LET'S GO AND DRESS ALL GANG-Y!

WAIT HERE, MONKEY.

PING!

ZING!

YEAH BOYYY!

HEE HEE! WE'RE SO GANG!

UMM...

WE'RE THE NAUGHTY CREW!

THAT'S A RUBBISH NAME.

NAUGHTY CREW!

DECEMBER

LOST IN THE SNOW!

SNOW FALLS ON THE WOODS, COVERING EVERYTHING IN A GENTLE WHITE BLANKET...

...BUT WHAT IS THAT LYING UNDERNEATH?

AAAARGH!
PLTHUH!

DID I DIE?

WHEN DID IT SNOW? I DON'T REMEMBER GETTING HERE. WHERE AM I? THAT WAS SOME PARTY.

DID I HAVE A PARTY?

EVERYONE'S PROBABLY FORGOTTEN ABOUT ME ALREADY.

DARN IT, MONKEY, **THINK**. WHAT'S THE LAST THING YOU REMEMBER?

HMM, BUNNY WAS HAVING A TEA PARTY, AND I TURNED UP ON A WICKED **JET SKI!**

HAR HAR!

WE HAD AN ARGUMENT, AND I STORMED OUT. I THINK HE CALLED ME A BUM FACE.

I REMEMBER IT WAS JUST STARTING TO SNOW.

BUT AFTER THAT, MY MIND IS A BLUR... SHRIEK!!

CHEMICAL X!

WOOSH WOOSH, THROUGH THE SNOW, A SLEDGING PIG IS ON THE GO...

LUCKY HE LOVES PLAYING IN IT, BECAUSE HE'LL FALL OFF ANY MINUTE...

THUNK!

SHRIEK!

NO! YOU STAY AWAY FROM THIS, PIG! IT IS NOT FOR YOU! NO!

NO! NOPE.

EE HEE HEE!

THIS... IS **CHEMICAL X!!** A MOST DANGEROUS AND UNIQUE SUBSTANCE!

TO PREVENT CATASTROPHE, IT MUST BE KEPT CHILLED!

WHICH IS WHY I HID IT IN THE SNOW.

WILL IT TURN ME INTO A BIG **CATERPILLAR?**

UMM, I DUNNO. MAYBE? YES.

COOOOL.

I MEAN **NO.** IT WON'T. GET AWAY!

HMM, WHY ARE YOU SO PROTECTIVE OF CHEMICAL X, SKUNKY? PERHAPS... IT IS WHAT **POWERS YOUR HIDEOUS CREATIONS?**

NO! ARGH!

I BET IT IS! IF WE TOOK THAT OFF YOU, YOU'D HAVE TO STOP DESTROYING THE WOODS!

I WANNA BE A CATERPILLAR!

UMM...

THE SMALL MATTER OF THE END OF THE WORLD!

ABOUT A YEAR AGO...

WHAT A LOVELY, PEACEFUL, DAY.

I WONDER HOW LONG IT'LL LAST.

BWOOOP!!!

SKUNKY! I'M YOU FROM THE FUTURE!

AT LAST! I KNEW I'D INVENT TIME TRAVEL!

HOW DID I DO IT? WAS THE SECRET INGREDIENT JELLY? I KNEW IT WAS JELLY!

YOU OBSERVED STASIS IN HIBERNATING... NO, WAIT, LISTEN! I DON'T HAVE LONG!

MY TIME TRAVEL WINDOW ONLY LASTS THIRTY SECONDS!

A YEAR FROM NOW, THE WOODS ARE RULED BY A **MONKEY!** HE DESTROYS EVERYTHING, ENSLAVES US ALL, AND TURNS LIFE INTO A **NIGHTMARE!!**

WHAT? DON'T BE SO SILLY. IF ANYONE WAS TO TAKE OVER, IT WOULD BE ME! I'M A GENIUS!

NOT IF HE GETS HIS HANDS ON YOUR TOP SECRET **DOOMSDAY DEVICE!**

GASP! HOW DID YOU KNOW ABOUT THAT?

I'M **YOU**. SHEESH! I'M NOT AS CLEVER AS I REMEMBER.

IN APPROXIMATELY ONE MINUTE, YOU ARE GOING TO MEET THIS MONKEY FOR THE FIRST TIME. YOU'LL SHOW HIM YOUR LABORATORY, WHERE HE'LL SEIZE CONTROL OF THE DOOMSDAY DEVICE!

USING IT TO TAKE OVER THE WOODS!

54

BUT I ONLY HAVE SECONDS LEFT HERE. HOW CAN I UNDO EVENTS AND SAVE THE FUTURE?

HELLO, MISTER SKUNKY. WE'RE TRYING TO BALANCE LEMON PUFF BISCUITS ON PIG'S HEAD.

NOT NOW, I AM TRYING TO USE MY GENIUS BRAIN!

ALTHOUGH, PERHAPS WHAT'S IN MY HEAD ISN'T THE SOLUTION. PERHAPS IT'S WHAT'S...ON YOURS!

SORRY! RIGHT NOW I NEED THIS MORE THAN YOU DO!

AWW, NOW WE HAVE TO START FROM THE BEGINNING!

A LEMON PUFF BISCUIT IS THE PERFECT SIZE TO BLOCK A CUSTOM Z-15 VENTILATION PIPE!

WEDGE!

PUTTING THE DOOMSDAY DEVICE OUT OF ACTION PERMANENTLY!

AND BACK, JUST IN TIME!

QUICKLY, ACTION BEAVER, USE THAT BRILLIANT MIND TO WORK OUT THE KEY CODE!

JAMIE

BZZZZZZ!

WAIT! NO! WHAT'S WRONG WITH IT?

NO! NOO!

BOOM!!

EIGHT MONTHS AGO...

I DID IT! I CHANGED THE FUTURE!

NOPE, THIS IS THE PAST. YOU WENT THE WRONG WAY.

AH, BUM. I'LL GO BACK TO THE FUTURE THEN.

JUST REMEMBER, PAST SKUNKY, MONKEY IS A DANGEROUS VARIABLE. SO ALWAYS KEEP HIM ENTERTAINED. ALWAYS DO WHAT HE SAYS...

BECAUSE WHILE YOU'RE BEHIND HIM, HE TAKES THE BLAME.

AND THEY WILL ALL BE TOO DISTRACTED TO NOTICE ME TAKING OVER THE WOODS...

BWOOP!!

..AND THEN THE WORLD!

THE PRESENT DAY...

SKUNKY! ARE YOU CAUSING TROUBLE?

ME? NO. NO.

BORING DAY.

NEXT TIME - "MERRY CHRISTMAS, MISTER MONKEY!"

57

~MERRY CHRISTMAS~ MISTER MONKEY!

'TWAS THE NIGHT BEFORE CHRISTMAS, AND EVERYONE IN THE WOODS WAS GETTING VERY EXCITED ABOUT THE FESTIVITIES TO COME. LITTLE REALISING THAT TONIGHT WAS THE NIGHT ALL OF THEIR LIVES WOULD CHANGE... **FOREVERRR!**

HAVE YOU TWO SEEN MONKEY?

NOPE! WE'VE BEEN HERE ALL NIGHT, DECORATING THE TREES WITH JELLY!

IT'S NOT JUST TONIGHT. I HAVEN'T SEEN HIM AROUND FOR THE LAST COUPLE OF WEEKS!

MAYBE YOU COULD ASK...

HE'S UP TO SOMETHING.

HUBBUB UBBUBBB!

PIG? ARE YOU OKAY?

HE'LL BE FINE. SOMETIMES HE REMEMBERS IT'S CHRISTMAS TOMORROW, AND HIS BRAIN <u>FUSES</u> WITH ALL THE EXCITEMENT!

HUBBUBB UBBUBB! UBB! UBB!

HUBBUBB UBBUBB! UBBB!

...UBBUBB... LE FOX, MAYBE HE'S SEEN MONKEY?

UMMM.

OKAY SURE, THANKS, PIG.

GIVE IT 3... 2... 1...

LE FOX? I DIDN'T EXPECT YOU TO GET INTO THE FESTIVE SPIRIT.

ZIS WAS NOT MY CHOICE. THAT STUPID SQUIRREL BRIBED ME WITH HIS DELICIOUS MINCE PIES.

HE PUTS A CHERRY ON TOP.

BUT IF ANYONE COMES NEAR ME, ASKING FOR PRESENTS, I'LL BITE THEM ON THE **BUMS.**

CHOMP!

OHHH-KAYY. LE FOX, HAVE YOU SEEN MONKEY?

HMM, NOT SINCE I BURIED HIM IN THE SNOW A WHILE AGO.

HE'S PROBABLY STILL LOST...

AS THE NARRATOR OF THIS CHRISTMAS TALE, I SHOULD INTERJECT THAT WE OBVIOUSLY SURVIVED, OTHERWISE I WOULDN'T BE TALKING TO YOU NOW. BUT I DID TELL YOU THAT ALL OUR LIVES WERE ABOUT TO CHANGE. AND THIS WAS THE EXACT MOMENT THAT HAPPENED, FOR ON THE EDGE OF THE WOODS WAS SOMETHING MANY OF US HAD NEVER ENCOUNTERED

HYOOOMANZ!

I CAN ONLY TELL YOU WHAT I KNOW - HUMANS ARE BIZARRE, SLOVENLY THINGS. THEY COME IN MANY SHAPES AND SIZES, GHOULISHLY DRIFTING FROM PLACE TO PLACE, MUMBLING TO THEMSELVES.

MAKING FARTY NOISES.

Frrpp!

HOW DO YOU KNOW SO MUCH ABOUT HUMANS, LE FOX?

I HAVE A COUSIN IN THE CITY. I HAVE SEEN MANY THINGS. ≥SHUDDER≥ MANY THINGS.

ISHMENT WOODS·

I DON'T THINK I'VE EVER SEEN A HUMAN BEFORE, BUT FOR SOME REASON THIS SEEMS FAMILIAR.

PAH! THOSE AREN'T HUMANS.

I COME FROM THE LAND OF HUMANS! BACK ON EARTH! THEY WEAR GLASSES AND BOW TIES AND FIRE ME INTO SPACE.

GOODNESS KNOWS WHAT YOU HAVE ON THIS PLANET.

SIGHHH. MONKEY, HOW MANY TIMES DO WE HAVE TO GO THROUGH THIS? YOU'RE STILL ON EARTH. YOU NEVER LEFT THE ATMOSPHERE!

HA! IF THAT'S TRUE, THEN WHERE ARE ALL THE TOILETS?

WE'RE ANIMALS! WE DON'T, UM... USE TOILETS. PFFT! EARTH HAS LOADS OF TOILETS. YOU CAN'T FOOL ME, WEIRD ALIEN CREATURES.

GRUHHHHH!

III AM A HYOOOMANZ! III SMELLS LIKE CHEZZ BOIGARS!!

GNUH! GNUH!

THIS IS WHAT I THOUGHT HUMANS LOOK LIKE. BIG, WEIRD, UGLY THINGS, THAT WE WOODLAND ANIMALS SHOULDN'T GO NEAR.

I'M SCARED JUST BEING ONE!

LOOK, THIS IS NEW FOR ALL OF US, BUT NOW WE HAVE DISCOVERED HUMANS EXIST, WE MUST BE CAREFUL NOT TO EXAGGERATE THINGS.

WE NEED TO ESTABLISH SOME FACTS.

FACTS? YOU WANT FACTS?

HERE'S A FACT. AVOID HUMANS.

WHAT DO YOU KNOW ABOUT HUMANS, SKUNKY? IT WAS YOU WHO RECOGNISED THEM AFTER ALL!

ME? OH, UH... NOTHING.

NOTHING AT ALL.

AHEM.

HE LIES! HE IS IN LEAGUE WITH THE HUMANS.

OH YEAH? WANNA TAKE THIS OUTSIDE, FOX?

NOW WHAT?

IT IS COLD OUT HERE.

LET'S GO BACK IN.

STOP BEING SO HYSTERICAL, BUNNY!

WHAT? I'M NOT.

WE ALL NEED TO CALM DOWN! AAARGH!

BANG! BANG!

HUH? WHASSAT?

THE HYOOOMANZ! THE HYOOOMANZ ARE COMING!

IT'S COMING FROM OUTSIDE!

GRAB!

BANG! BANG!

WELL, WHATEVER HUMANS ARE, MAYBE IF WE STAY OUT OF THEIR WAY THEY'LL LEAVE US ALONE.

PLANS FOR DEMOLITION -OF CRINKLEWOODS- AND BUILDING OF MOTORWAY

END OF YEAR ONE AND BOOK TWO! SEE YOU SOOOON!

JAMIE

63

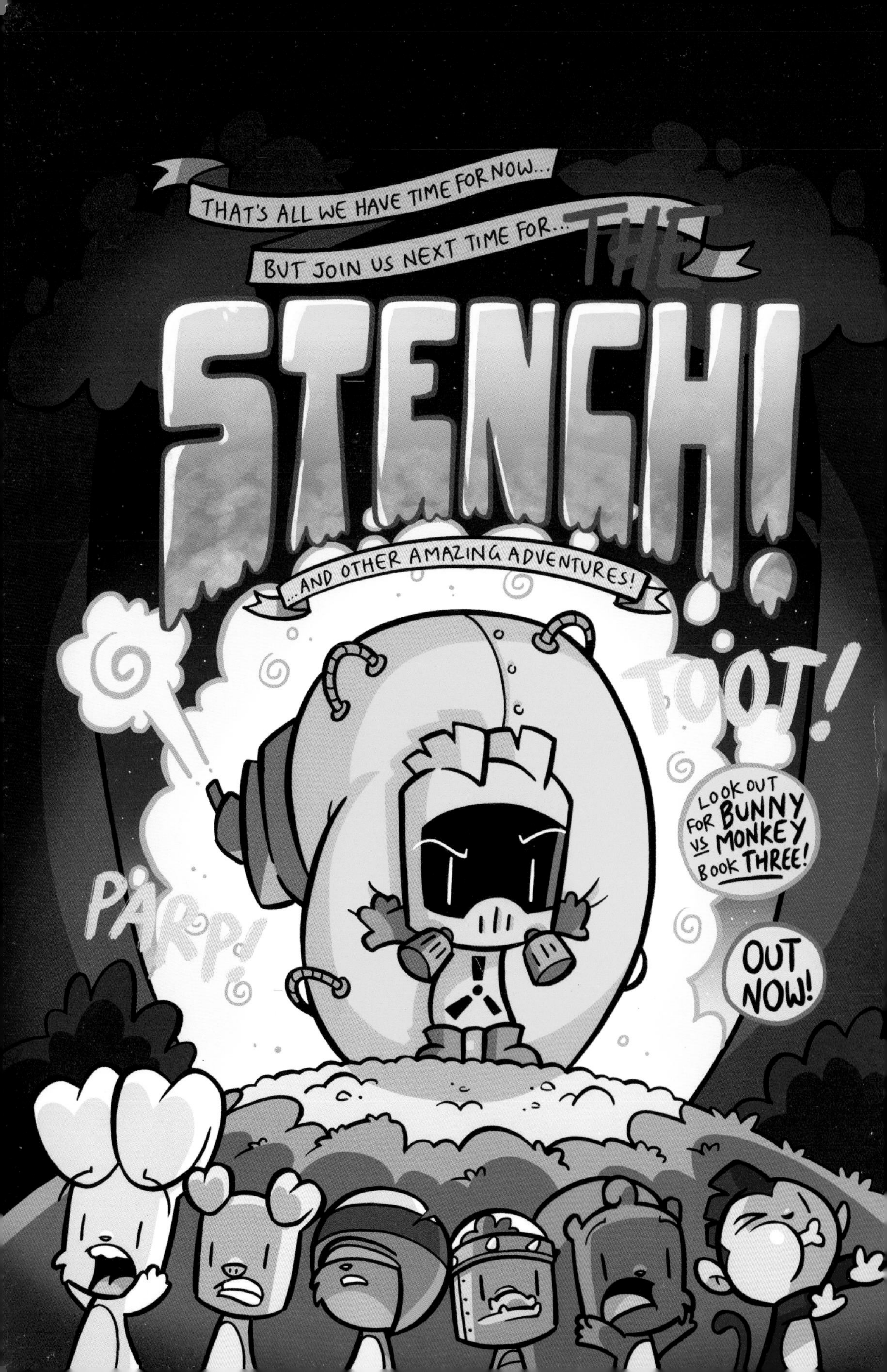

THAT'S ALL WE HAVE TIME FOR NOW...
BUT JOIN US NEXT TIME FOR...
THE STENCH!
...AND OTHER AMAZING ADVENTURES!
TOOT!
LOOK OUT FOR BUNNY VS MONKEY BOOK THREE!
PARP!
OUT NOW!